DESIRABLE

frank cottrell boyce

With illustrations by

Cate James

Barrington Stoke

First published in 2008 in Great Britain by
Barrington Stoke Ltd
18 Walker Street, Edinburgh, EH3 7LP

www.barringtonstoke.co.uk

This edition first published 2014
Reprinted 2016, 2018, 2019, 2020

Text © 2008 Frank Cottrell-Boyce
Illustrations © 2014 Cate James

A CIP catalogue record for this book is available
from the British Library upon request

ISBN: 978-1-78112-424-6

Printed in Great Britain by Charlesworth Press

This book has dyslexia-friendly features

For Joe, Chiara and Denny – explicably popular

Contents

1

How Not to Party

You won't believe this but I used to be a
loser.

Like one time it was my birthday and
Mum said, "Let's have a bit of a party,
George. Ask anyone you like." And I couldn't
get anyone to come. Not one person. I did
ask Tiny Biggs, from the Warhammer Club
at school, because he's a loser too. He said,
"Will there be food?"

"Loads of food. Chicken wings. Hula
Hoops. Birthday cake."

"Sounds good."

"So you'll come?"

"Can't. Sorry."

"Why not?"

"Social suicide, isn't it? If anyone found out I'd been to your house, I'd be a joke. No offence."

Tiny won't sit with me at lunch time for the same reason. The only time he talks to me is during Warhammer Club. That's because there are only two people in the Warhammer Club – me and him.

Tiny thinks that things are going to be different in the future. "Girls are obsessed with fashion," he says. "And celebs. All we need is for Kylie to say she likes Warhammer, and the next thing you know, we'll be fighting the women off."

So far, Kylie has issued no Warhammer-related statement, so it's still just the two of us.

There's a girl who gets the same bus as me called Daniella Gallagher. I thought about asking her to my party too. I thought about it in great detail, in fact. I knew I wouldn't be able to ask her just like that. I haven't spoken to a girl since Year 5, except in self-defence.

But I did work out a plan. If I dropped my bag just as I was getting on the bus, she might spot the birthday card that I'd carefully left sticking out of the side pocket and she might say, "Oh. Is it your birthday? Are you having a party or anything?"

And then I'd say, "My mum's gonna cook a big tea – chicken wings, birthday cake, stuff like that."

And she'd say, "Stop, stop. You're making me hungry."

And I'd say, "Come and get some if you like. There'll be plenty to spare."

And she'd say, "Brilliant!" and come home with me. And we'd all live happily ever after.

I wrote the whole thing down on a piece of paper and learned it off by heart, so I'd be ready.

And it nearly worked, too. The bus did come. I did drop the bag. But then Daniella

didn't look down and see the card. She just
stepped over the bag and got on the bus.

That slowed me down when I was picking
things up. By the time I stood up, the bus
was moving off with Daniella on board and I
got left at the bus stop.

So my birthday sit-off was just me and Mum and Dad and Grandad. Mum said, "Well, this is cosy."

"It's great," said Grandad. "Can we do the birthday cake now?"

Dad said, "We haven't even had the chicken wings yet!"

"I know," said Grandad. "But I've got to go in a minute. I'm having my hair cut."

Even my own grandad didn't want a sit-off with me on my birthday.

Mum lit the candles.

Grandad said, "Do you remember your Patrick's birthday, and you said he could have five friends and fifty turned up?"

Patrick is my big brother. He's at uni. He's very popular. And clever. And good at football. And drawing. And piano.

"And then, when it was time for the cake, he took a napkin, put it in front of the cake, blew and then ... the whole cake vanished!"

He's also good at magic tricks.

"How did he do that?" said Grandad.

And Patrick's good at Maths. And fixing things. And talking to people. I don't know how he does it. Any of it. I don't know how he gets top grades, scores goals, makes friends. These things are all as weird as vanishing cakes to me.

"I got you a present," said Grandad, passing me a little parcel. "Go on, open it. My haircut's not going to wait for ever."

I opened it. I'd been hinting like mad for some extra Warhammer figures, so it was a big surprise to find that the parcel contained a bottle of aftershave with a pair of "free limited edition cuff-links" stuck to the lid.

Grandad said, "I hope you like it. Got to go." And went.

"Nice cuff-links," said Dad. "Just what every boy needs."

The aftershave was called "Desirable".

This aftershave BBE August 1982

Mum said, "I bought him that aftershave when I was a little girl."

"And they're still making it? It must be good then. It must be a classic," said Dad.

"I don't mean I bought him that brand. I mean I bought him that bottle. Look on the back."

On the back was a sticker of a man with big hair and a droopy moustache. Under that it said, "This aftershave best before end: August 1982."

Mum said, "Give it to me. I'll put it in the recycling."

I said, "No. Don't. Maybe it's like wine or something. Maybe the longer you leave it, the better it gets."

"I wouldn't risk it if I were you," said Dad. "Here's our present to you."

And they gave me the exact Warhammer figures that I'd always wanted.

2

How to Wear Aftershave

When I woke up the next morning, the sun was shining on the line of Warhammer goblins I'd arranged on the window sill, and on the bottle of aftershave which I'd left next to them.

The aftershave threw lemon splashes of sunlight all over the room. I took the bottle and waggled it around for a while, making the lemon splashes dash around the walls. I was pretending it was some kind of wizard torch thing. I picked the limited edition cuff-links off the lid. Then I tried to open the

bottle. The stopper wouldn't budge at first.
I had to grip it with the edge of the duvet and
twist it. Then suddenly it came free.

The second the lid was off, Mrs Doyle's
dog started barking. There was a fluttery
racket in the garden as all the birds in
the trees seemed to take off at once. Cats
meowed. And Mum banged on my bedroom
wall. She shouted, "What's going on in
there?"

An aftershave you could smell through
walls! I thought I'd better not try it. So I
stuck the lid back on and shoved the bottle
under my bed. But a bit of the liquid had
spilled on my fingers. I rubbed that into my
cheeks. It stung like a really angry jellyfish.

When I got to school, Perfect Paula was hanging round the Year 10 entrance with her mates, same as every morning.

Every morning I have to walk past her while she entertains her crew by making hilarious comments about me, my clothes, and most of all my backpack. (Mum makes me use this fluorescent yellow backpack for health and safety reasons.)

As I walked towards Paula, I could see her grinning as if she'd thought of something really bad. I put my head down and got ready to ignore her. Then suddenly her face changed. She sniffed the air like a nervous dog, and then she said, "Hello, George. Nice to see you. Are you going to registration?"

It was 8.50. Where did she think I was going? Ballroom dancing? I said, "Yes."

"Can I come with you? No. I know, let's all go."

And they all followed me in through the main doors, giggling and nudging each other.

Paula said, "George, what are you doing after this?"

"I.T."

"George is doing I.T. Let's all do I.T."

I said, "I think you'll find it's on the timetable. You're doing I.T. whether you want to or not."

"Oh, I love the way he says things! Don't you love the way he says things – all snotty and sarcastic."

They followed me into school.

It was a trap. I knew that. I knew they were only nice to me when they wanted to lull me into a false sense of security. They were probably planning to pull me into the girls' toilets and remove my eyebrows with a pair of tweezers. Or something. It had to be a trap.

But it was a nice trap.

Most days, when I walk around the corridors in our school, I try to stick as close to the walls as I can. I try to think myself invisible. Today I was not invisible. Today I was totally visible. I was walking in the middle of the corridor, surrounded by girls. I couldn't help enjoying it, even if I was worried about what they were planning. Maybe a fish thinks the bait tastes nice, even if it has got a hook in it.

Our form teacher is Mrs Dudman. In all the years I've been at the school she's only said one sentence to me. She said, "Stop talking, George."

Today when I walked in, Mrs Dudman looked at me, did that worried-dog sniff thing that Paula had done, and said, "Hello,

George, you look nice today. Have you done something different to your hair?"

I've never done anything to my hair. Except wash it after swimming on Wednesdays and after karate on Sundays. I said, "No, Miss." But no one heard me. They were all discussing the niceness of my hair.

Tiny Biggs stared at me in amazement.

Things got even weirder in I.T.

Mr Fitton didn't do the worried-dog sniff or make comments about my hair. He told us all to split into groups of 3. There are 28 people in my class. Most days, if we split into groups of 3, it means 9 groups of 3 – and me on my own.

Today, Mr Fitton had just finished talking when Perfect Paula slid her chair in on one side of me and Daniella slid hers in on the other side. Jade McKinnon came and stood too close to Daniella.

"I always work with Paula," Jade said.

"Yes, she always works with me," Paula agreed.

"I want to work with George," said Daniella.

"Well, George doesn't want to work with you, do you, George?" said Paula. "Tell her to get lost, George."

I turned to Daniella. No way was I going to tell her to get lost. If I'd said anything it would have been, "Please don't get lost." But when I opened my mouth, nothing came out.

Daniella glared at me, got up and went and sat with Mr Fitton. I tried to say, "No, wait, come back ..." but that didn't come out either.

3

How to Be Popular with Girls

The I.T. lesson was about making websites. Each group had to design a fan site for a band or a singer, and decide what to put on the front page and how to lay it out.

Paula leaned over to Jade and said, "We're doing a George fan site. It's called WeLoveGeorge and it's going to have loads of George gossip and George facts on it. George, what's your favourite colour?"

"I don't really have a favourite colour."

"Write that down," Paula said. "George is open to all colours. Because he looks good in everything. Like that bag he's got – the one that looks like radio-active custard."

"Yeah."

"It's so cool."

"My fluorescent backpack is cool?" I said. "How come you never said that before?"

"I never really noticed before. Can I take a picture of you?" Jade said.

The two of them then started taking pictures of me with their mobiles.

By now, time was up and Mr Fitton said, "OK, let's hear some of your ideas ... Jasmine."

Jasmine's group was her twin sister, Amber, and another girl, and she said, "Our idea was to have a fan site all about George."

"That was our idea," said Paula.

"And ours," said Maddie Yates.

Every single girl was working on a
George Owusu (i.e. Me) fan site. All except
Daniella. She – amazingly – was working on
a Warhammer site.

I said, "Warhammer? That's interesting."

"Not as interesting as you, George," said
Perfect Paula.

"We were going to do, like – 20 Things You
Didn't Know About George," said Lucy Begley.
"Like his favourite colour ..."

"George doesn't have a favourite colour,"
said Paula, smugly.

"Well, his favourite book then."

"*The Lord of the Rings*," said Maddie. "Isn't that right, George?"

"Well ... I suppose so ..." I said.

Tiny Biggs looked bewildered. Angry Al Kominski looked like he was going to explode. "What's going on?" he roared. "What. Is. Going. On? Someone tell me now before I get angry."

No one wants Angry Al to get angry, so Mr Fitton said, "Yes, George, what is going on? Is this some kind of joke?"

"I don't know, sir."

"You don't know?"

"No, sir."

"Well perhaps you'd better find out. Go and report to the Head of Year. Now."

Mrs Hardman is supposed to be our Head of Year, but most of the time she is obsessed with raising money for the new sports hall. If you're ever in trouble, you can get out of it by giving her some money for her sports hall fund. She didn't even look up when I first came in. She just said, "Are you in trouble?"

"Not sure, Miss."

"Got any money on you?"

"Only my bus fare, Miss."

"Hmmm, then I expect you're probably in a lot of ..." She stopped. She sniffed. She smiled at me. A big, glowing smile. It melted over her face like butter over a hot crumpet. "Oh," she said. "It's ..."

"Owusu, Miss. George Owusu."

"George Owusu. How lovely to see you. What can I get you? Biscuit? Cup of tea?

Coffee? I think we've got hot chocolate somewhere."

"Mr Fitton sent me to see you, Miss."

"Did he? I must remember to thank him." She'd already started making the hot chocolate.

"I haven't got time for chocolate, Miss," I said. "I've got double Maths now."

"Oh, don't go."

"I've got to, Miss. Maths is so important."

By lunch time, I knew this wasn't a trap. By lunch time, I knew that everyone just loved me. When I tried to sit at my usual table – the one with the wobbly leg, by the bins – it was already surrounded. Paula and her mates, Jasmine and Amber, they were all there. Then there was a bit of a row because they didn't all fit.

Things got worse when the Year 8 girls wanted to sit by me too. And the Year 9s.

In the end, someone went and got Mrs Hardman and she worked out a rota so that all the girls could take turns sitting next to me. "And it's my go first," she said.

The only girl who didn't want to sit with me was Daniella. She was at the opposite side of the hall, near the climbing wall, eating her lunch and reading a book, all on her own.

It was only when I saw her doing that today that I realised I'd seen her doing it before – lots of times – that she often ate on her own.

Angry Al came over and said, "I want a word with you."

Mrs Hardman said, "Have you booked?"

"Booked?"

"You have to book to sit near to George," Mrs Hardman told him. "These places are reserved from now until Christmas. I can put your name down if you like."

Angry Al clutched his head. "What. Is. Going. On?" he howled. "It's confusing me. Why is he so popular all of a sudden?"

"I don't know," said Mrs Hardman. "I think he's just bloomed, really. George, do you think you've bloomed?"

"I suppose so," I said.

Well, I wasn't going to tell them, was I, that it was all down to a bottle of aftershave that was more than 30 years past its sell-by date.

4

How to Recognise Goblins

Next morning I lay in bed, thinking what a great day that was. And today would be just as good. And tomorrow. And every day. All I had to do was dab on a bit of Grandad's old aftershave. So I did.

As soon as I opened the bottle, Mrs Doyle's dog started barking, the birds all flew off and Mum banged on my wall. I dabbed a bit behind my ears, then I wrapped the bottle in a T-shirt and put it in my school bag. I wasn't going to leave it in the house and risk Mum dumping it in the recycling.

Two minutes later the doorbell rang and there was Lucy Begley on the doorstep. And Jasmine. And her sister, Amber. And Maddie Yates. And, well, a lot of girls.

Hi, George!" they all said together. "Are you coming to school?"

"It's a school day, so yes I am going to school."

"He's being sarcastic again," said Maddie. "I love it!"

"So do we!" said a whole bunch of other girls. "And look what we've got!" They all turned their backs towards me. They were all wearing fluorescent yellow backpacks.

"We've got that George Owusu look," said Jasmine.

Dad was passing the front door in his pyjamas. All the girls waved at him, yelling, "There's George's dad, look! Hello, George's dad!"

"Errm," said Dad. "Hello." He waved back, a bit nervous.

Then he hissed at me, "What's going on? How come you're so popular all of a sudden?"

"What a silly question," said Mum. "He's popular because he's lovely."

"Well, yeah," said Dad. "But he wasn't popular before."

"Ah. Well. Now that did puzzle me," said Mum. "If you'd asked me then why he wasn't popular, we could have discussed it. But why's he popular? Because he's lovely. End of."

Dad didn't look as if he believed her. I just shrugged and went to school. Jasmine let me walk under her umbrella. Amber carried my bag. Maddie told me little jokes she'd saved up just for me. It was lovely.

I said, "Why can't everyone's walk to school be like this?"

Jasmine said, "Not everyone's like you, George."

It was a shame we didn't get all the way to school. But Perfect Paula's mum stopped in her big pink Audi and offered me a lift, and it seemed rude to say no.

"Sit in the back with me," said Paula.

"No. In the front with me," said her mum.

"In the back with me."

In the end they decided that I would go in the back as far as the lights and in the front the rest of the way to school.

While they were arguing, I looked out of the window and saw Tiny Biggs standing at the kerb, waiting to cross. I was going to wave to him but Perfect Paula's mum drove through a puddle and soaked him, so I slid down in my seat in case he saw me.

That's when I thought – hang on, I'm a celeb. We don't need to wait for Kylie. I can make Warhammer popular all by myself.

"What are you thinking, George?" said Paula.

"I'm thinking I might go to Warhammer Club this lunch time," I said.

When I got to Warhammer Club that lunch time, Tiny was jumping up and down with happiness.

"It's happened," he said. "I don't know how. But it's happened. Warhammer is in. Come and look."

The I.T. room was packed with girls. As soon as I walked in, they all screamed and waved.

"I've died," said Tiny. "And gone to Heaven."

I said, "Who'd like to play Warhammer?"

"We would!!!!!!!!" they all yelled.

"And so would I," said a voice at the door.
It was Mrs Hardman.

And a voice behind her said, "And me." It was Perfect Paula's mum. "You don't mind me spending the day in school, I hope," she said to Mrs Hardman. "It's just that, well, George is here."

So, me and Tiny played one game to show them how it worked. Every time I threw the dice, they all cheered and shouted, "Go, George!"

Tiny said this was annoying, but I thought it was great. Then Maddie put her hand up and asked a question about goblins. I tried my best to explain the difference between a goblin and an orc. Then I told them some more about the nature and geography of the

Warhammer World, stuff like that. The girls seemed really interested. They all sat in a circle and stared up at me while I talked.

I forgot all about lunch until Mr Fitton came in and said, "What are you girls doing in here? This is supposed to be Warhammer Club."

"We are the Warhammer Club," said the girls.

"For ever," added Lucy in a dreamy voice.

"I don't know what's going on," said Mr Fitton. "But I do know that you've only got ten minutes left for lunch."

When we got to the dining hall, they'd set up all the tables so they made one big table down the middle of the room, and everyone could sit with me. My old table was still over in the corner by the bins though, and Daniella was sitting at it. With Tiny Biggs. He must have left Warhammer Club early. I hadn't even seen him go.

Don't get me wrong. It was great sitting on that big table, with everyone passing me food and telling me jokes. But every now and then I looked over at my old table and thought how lucky Tiny was to have Daniella to himself like that.

5

How to Be Unpopular with Boys

Then it was Games.

When I walked into the changing rooms,
Angry Al Kominski was waiting for me with
Tiny and another boy I'd never seen before.
He was huge. And I suddenly realised that
the boys' changing rooms were probably
the only place in the whole school where I
wouldn't have girls to protect me.

I said, "Hi."

"This," said Angry Al, pointing to the huge boy, "is my friend, Huge Arnold. He doesn't go to this school. But he is Perfect Paula's boyfriend. He wants to know why she's got pictures of you on her mobile. And on her bedroom wall."

"On her bedroom wall? Really?" I said.

"Grrrrr," said Huge Arnold.

"We're playing rugby today," said Angry Al. "And Huge Arnold has agreed to play with us. Even though he doesn't go to this school. He's going to play on my team. Against you."

Huge Arnold said "Grrrrr" again. He didn't need to say anything else. "Grrrrr" said it all really.

"Just tell us what's going on," said Tiny. "Tell us how you do it, so we can do it too."

He was looking at my bag as he said this.

I clutched it a bit tighter. I suppose that's what gave the game away.

I really think I might have told Tiny the truth there and then – if Mr Fitton hadn't come in just then and said, "Right. Get changed. Let's play rugby."

I said, "Please, sir, I'm excused, sir."

"Excused why?"

I hadn't really thought of a reason. But I had thought of a powerful ally. I said, "Honest, sir. I am excused – ask Mrs Hardman."

"It was Mrs Hardman's idea, George."

"What?"

"She seemed to think the sight of you running round in shorts would be very popular. She sold tickets."

"What?"

"For the Sports Hall Fund," Mr Fitton said. "The whole school is out there ready to cheer you on. They've paid two quid a head. So no, you can't be excused."

"I can't even play rugby."

"Well, it's time to learn."

I got changed and put my clothes in my backpack. I tried to push the bottle even further down into the bottom, but all the time Tiny was watching me and the more I tried to hide it, the more he suspected something.

"OK," said Mr Fitton. "Is everyone ready? Tiny, you're excused for being tiny. Angry Al ..."

"Let me play, sir."

"No can do I'm afraid. Your personality is a health and safety risk."

So off we went. A huge cheer went up when I walked onto the pitch. It should have been a thrill, but I was too worried about what was going on in the changing room.

About two minutes into the match, there was a kind of mighty fluttering sound and from every tree for miles around flocks of birds flew up into the sky and headed for the changing rooms. Dogs barked. Cats meowed. And the head of every girl swivelled towards the school.

I knew then that Tiny had opened the aftershave. Two minutes later, the birds flew off, the dogs stopped barking, and the girls started watching me again.

It wasn't until half-time that I found out what had happened. Angry Al had tried to get the aftershave off Tiny. Tiny had tried to run and hide in the showers. There was a

struggle. The bottle broke. The aftershave
all vanished down the drain.

It was all over.

6

How to Be Lucky

I asked Mum where she'd bought the aftershave, thinking maybe the shop might have some left.

"Barney's Bargains on Croft Road," she said. "It was knocked down to make way for the mega Tesco." Mum works at the Tesco. She said, "I often think of that shop. It would have been just in the middle of aisle 7 – where the pasta sauces and Mexican ready-meals are now."

I searched the internet. "Desirable" is not a good word to google.

It was all over.

Or maybe it wasn't. When you thought about it, it was mad to think that a splash of aftershave could change your life. Maybe I had just bloomed. Maybe it was nothing to do with the aftershave.

When Jasmine and Amber got on the bus next morning, I sat up and smiled at them. Then I shuffled along the seat so that they could sit by me.

Jasmine looked at me and shuddered. Amber said, "There's George."

Jasmine said, "And your point is?"

"Nothing," said her sister and they sat at the back.

I could hear Jasmine saying, "I wonder what they ever saw in him."

When Daniella got on at the next stop, the only seat left on the bus was the one next to me. "Hi," I said and smiled at her when she sat down.

"Oh you'll talk to me now," she said. "Now that no one else wants to."

"How do you know that no one talks to me?"

"I'm a girl. Girls communicate with each other." She showed me a text from Paula to everyone in the school. "George Owusu," it said, "is SOOOOO over."

"But you don't do what the other girls do," I said. "You're different. So you could talk to me."

"I could but I don't want to. You've changed."

"Yes, I have changed," I said. "And before I changed you wouldn't talk to me."

"Before you changed, you wouldn't talk to me."

"Yeah, but I wanted to. I really wanted to."

"You say that."

"I can prove it."

I rummaged around in my bag and found the piece of paper with the notes written on it – the notes about what I was going to say to Daniella on my birthday.

"It was your birthday?" she said. "You never said."

"I never said anything. But I wanted to."

She was reading the notes. Suddenly I
was embarrassed about it, so I got off the bus
a stop early. While I was waiting to cross the
road, Perfect Paula's big pink Audi went past
and splashed me.

That lunch time, though, Daniella came to
Warhammer.

"This," said Tiny, "could be the start of
something big."

It was the start of three people playing Warhammer instead of two. And three people having lunch together afterwards instead of sitting on their own. It was the start of swapping books and sharing playlists with each other, and going to the pictures on Saturday afternoons. It was friendship. It was great.

In the week before we broke up for Christmas it was even buying presents and cards for people who were not your mum and dad. I got a goblin captain for Tiny and another one for Daniella. I painted hers to make it a bit special. Tiny bought me and Daniella an orcish canon each. He'd painted hers to make it special.

Daniella bought Tiny a mounted goblin. But she bought me something different. She said, "I know it's a bit old looking. I got it in Demented Discounts. I remembered you having something like it months ago."

It was a bottle of Desirable. Best before 1982. "Thanks," I said. "It's what I always wanted."

This aftershave B&G August 1992

It was the school Winter Warmer that
night – a kind of party with dancing in the
gym, hot dogs in the yard and a casino in the
I.T. room – to raise funds for the new sports
hall.

Going home that night with a full bottle
of Desirable in my bag, I found myself
thinking how great it would be to walk in
there and have every girl smiling at me, like
in the old days. All it would take was one
drop.

Everyone got dressed up for it. Mum even bought me a new shirt. It had no buttons on the cuffs.

"I know," she said. "It's meant to be like that. You wear it with cuff-links, like the ones your grandad bought you."

"But, Mum, they look stupid. And they've got 'Lucky' written on them! Just think what people are going to say!"

I was going to look even more stupid than ever at the party. All the more reason to splash on the Desirable. I was just about to open the bottle when Tiny and Daniella turned up in Tiny's mum's car.

"Look at Daniella, one girl with two boys," said Mum.

"Nice to be popular," said Dad.

Then Mum sighed. "Remember when our George was popular?" she asked.

That fixed it for me. I stuffed the bottle into my pocket and made up my mind to smother myself in it as soon as I got to school.

The gym looked amazing when we got there – a great big tree twinkled in the corner, festoons of tinsel hung from the climbing wall, and the lights kept changing all the time from gold to blue to red. And couples were dancing together.

"This is going to be great," said Tiny, rubbing his hands.

And suddenly I knew what I wanted.

I didn't want every girl in the place asking me to dance. I wanted Daniella all to myself. But what about Tiny?

Easy.

When we went outside to buy some hot dogs, I slipped the lid off the bottle in my pocket. For a moment, the music stopped and you could hear birds beating around the outside of the building. I rubbed my finger round the rim and then wiped it on the back of Tiny's neck before putting the lid back on.

When we got back into the gym, every head in the place swivelled to look at us.

"Oh, no," groaned Daniella. "Please don't tell me you're back in fashion."

I said, "I don't think it's me."

And every girl in the place screeched, "Tiny!!!!!" and ran over to try to get him to dance.

In the end, one of the teachers had to get a clipboard and come up with a list so that he could dance with everyone. I have never seen anyone so happy.

Apart from me and Daniella. We
danced – in a rubbish way, but still – and we
talked. And later on we went into the casino.

"Only a pound a chip for a game of
roulette," said Mrs Hardman. "All the money
is going to the new sports hall."

We bought three chips and put them on
red and won!

We put those on black and won again.
And again. And then on red again. We just
couldn't stop winning.

"Let's be a bit more daring," said Daniella.
"Pick a number."

So we put everything on 16. And we won.

We had 500 chips by this stage. Daniella was jumping up and down with excitement. "Don't worry, Mrs Hardman," she said. "We'll split the winnings with the school."

It was as I was raking the chips in that I noticed something. My cuff-links. My lucky cuff-links. Could it be the cuff-links that were doing this? No. But then again, maybe.

Daniella said, "Let's take the money and stop now."

But I had this prickly feeling in my wrists, just where the cuff-links were touching them. "No," I said. "We're putting all 500 on 23 to win."

Mrs Hardman turned a bit pale. Then she spun the roulette wheel and dropped the ball into the wheel ...

Are you desirable ...
Or are you a loser?

Have you got what it takes to be explicably popular?
Test yourself with these questions and find out!

(1) When you started big school did they ...

- ☐ **A.** Get your name right?
- ☐ **B.** Get your name wrong?
- ☐ **C.** Re-name the school after you?

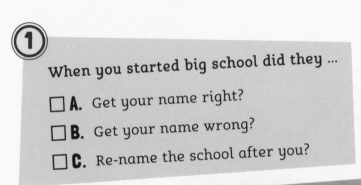

(2) Do you walk to school ...

- ☐ **A.** With friends?
- ☐ **B.** All alone?
- ☐ **C.** Pursued by paparazzi?

(3) When you walk into a classroom do people generally ...

- ☐ **A.** Carry on doing what they were doing?
- ☐ **B.** Hide under the desks or run for the fire exit?
- ☐ **C.** Applaud?

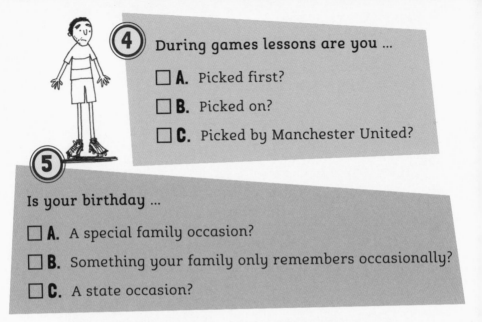

4 During games lessons are you ...

☐ **A.** Picked first?

☐ **B.** Picked on?

☐ **C.** Picked by Manchester United?

5 Is your birthday ...

☐ **A.** A special family occasion?

☐ **B.** Something your family only remembers occasionally?

☐ **C.** A state occasion?

6 You buy a new shirt. Do people say ...

☐ **A.** That shirt is sick?

☐ **B.** That shirt makes me feel sick?

☐ **C.** Alas my heart is sickening for a shirt just like yours?

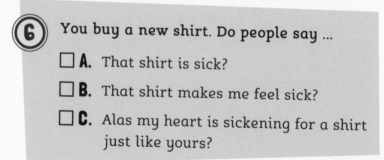

If you answered
MOSTLY A ...
You have nothing to worry about.

If you answered
MOSTLY B ...
Don't worry, you might well grow up to be a genius.

If you answered
MOSTLY C ...
You are probably lying.

Our books are tested
for children and young people by
children and young people.

Thanks to everyone who consulted on
a manuscript for their time and effort in
helping us to make our books better
for our readers.